'Clown World'

A book by
Dale Wayne Colgrove

Dale Wayne Colgrove

ISBN: 978-1-964283-89-0

Book Writing Founders

This little book recognizes every Clown, real or not, and is dedicated to Human imagination and the Creative Process.

Table of Contents

About the Author

Dale Colgrove, now residing in Palm Springs, California, is a retired school band director from Texas and the author of this first published book, Clown World. Beyond his identity as a musician, Dale is a seasoned entertainment professional whose career showcases remarkable versatility and commitment. His love for music has led to the creation of over 500 sound recordings, encompassing a diverse portfolio that includes Hollywood productions, dynamic live performances, and innovative video projects. His experience ranges from performing at Knott's Berry Farm with his band to sharing the stage with the legendary Dick Clark at the Dallas Adolphus, as well as lending his voice to animated projects and hosting live radio broadcasts. Notably, he has had the honor of performing with the esteemed Les Paul Trio in New York City and collaborating with a symphonic orchestra in Southern California, further establishing his reputation as a true master of his craft.

Chapter One

Jeremy Bigham was a nine-year-old-boy whose greatest aspiration in his young life was to become a clown someday – a professional circus clown.

Jeremy had already become familiar with the clowns because prior to his birth, his father had owned and operated a small but successful, nontraveling, three-ring circus with a midway carnival.

It was located near a town called Baraboo.

This town was famous for its circuses and traveling tent shows.

Entertainers of all skills, exhibition and physical oddity could be found both on the circus midway and in the rings. Acrobats, tumblers, and wild animal tamers would appear.

But, probably since the hour of his birth, it was the clowns of the circus who occupied a special place in Jeremy's heart.

Martha

Jeremy's mother was a quiet woman, generally liked by most. However, to some, it had been expressed the belief that she had been keeping a secret: Something unspoken nor otherwise expressed.

Comments over her facial appearance, especially concerning her nose and lower lip, were common. She had been criticized by some women of her church congregation over the volumes of make-up she employed.

She had once been a nurse, so when confronted, Martha would rely upon her knowledge of medical terms to lay claim to a certain, unfortunate physical disorder: She referred to, 'Rosacea,' which is a skin pigmentation anomaly where the sufferer is marked with red because of a malfunction in the melanin.

Her nose and lip were quite crimson. Yes, red, indeed! And the nose, quite bulbous.

Also, her feet were exceptionally large.

These things, along with exceedingly arched eyebrows, made her persona appear somewhat exaggerated.

Jeremy saw little of his mother during the day, as he was in school while she was at church, leaving just after breakfast to provide cooking, general mending and sewing. After lunch, she would spend time balancing the circus books, then just before nightfall, she'd go out to collect the day's take from the midway.

Jeremy held an abstract respect for his mother. Her attitude toward him was often trite and unreasonable.

She held little regard for his personal possessions and would often demonstrate indifference toward his independent interests.

It was common for her to enter Jeremy's room without his knowledge and take some of his treasures to the garbage.

Family heirlooms meant nothing to her.

She confiscated and disposed of sentimental letters, vintage baby clothing, or photographic film recordings—mementos retained to give the nod to the past or illumination upon family history.

Kate

Jeremy's older sister, Kate, was a brattish tattle-tail, with an exceptional talent for gossip and general, subversive rabble-rousing. Deceptive was her flattering appearance.

Orange-red hair, yellow and blue-on-white, petty coated dresses, green, flashing butterfly eyes. A wee, devilish nature lay behind a sly, Cheshire cat-like grin, seemingly there only while the owner contemplates some scheme involving downright charlatanry or clandestine debauchery.

Jeremy's dark, curly hair mirrored his father's, as did his general attire.

In conservative contrast to his sister, he never appeared without a pressed shirt with a vest, tie and polished shoes.

Having a knack at playing the harmonica, Jeremy's instrument could be seen poking from his vest pocket, keeping its use close within his reach, ready for immediate employ.

Julius

Jeremy's father could be somewhat of a curmudgeon, delighting in the muse of making serious affairs over hardly consequential drama. Insults often accompanied by compliments.

Joy, for him, was found in the preservation of communal agreement through his mandate.

His children trusted him and felt benefit through their being the children of Julius Bigham, owner of the circus.

There were times when the family sat together to dine around their modest but formal table positioned behind tall French doors in a room located at the end of a long hallway.

Julius would suggest that Mother go and powder her nose while he smokes his cigar. Jeremy noticed these occurrences and, after careful, mature-for-nine observation, began to make correlation between the smoking of the cigar and the powdering of the nose…like an unspoken responsive signal.

Julius would take out a cigar (a slim Churchill, hand-rolled), put it in his mouth, then take a wooden match from his vest pocket, strike it on the heel of his boot and after puffs of blue, an expertly designed smoke ring would grow bigger with its ascension before it would disappear into the Either.

Watching his father smoke, Jeremy would silently wish for one of his father's cigars to suddenly explode!

Jeremy dreamed of doing such things, but he questioned himself as to whether he could actually do them. As he decided he might, he couldn't expect a gleeful reaction from his father, for Glee, originating from his father, was something he found near impossible to imagine.

Julius Bigham was at this time in his early forties. His background as a businessman was notorious, having a general reputation as a greedy man with a surly disposition hidden under an extremely well-mannered veil.

Eloquent language, gentlemanly mannerisms and exquisite dress became a disguise, with a face curled from a general disgust for things considered impractical.

He did not particularly enjoy the circus business. Acquiring wealth and recognition was his primary motivation, which was adequately met by monthly circus revenue.

He did enjoy being in the focus of the spotlight, acting as head ringmaster, being neatly dressed in sequin-tailed vests with matching top-hats and knee-high riding boots.

As he spoke, a large, commanding bass-to-baritone vocal prowess came forth from his mouth, amplified by employing the aid of a special device he held in his hand:

A 'Sengerphone': an acoustic megaphone-like device used by the Germans during the war. Because of its design, with the mouth and nose both being completely covered while speaking, one's voice could be heard over very long distances.

Henry Barnes

Henry Barnes was a benevolent man with a genuine love of people and a devoted, internal joy imparted through the process of making folks smile.

In his former life, he had been a professional animal trainer.

Henry had owned an interest in his great uncle's circus, the 'Barnes Bonanza.' It was a typical Wild-West Show, employing mostly horses, cows and various barnyard foul. Mixed in were some exotic animals:

One skinny elephant, an old, toothless lion and a crippled, mangy tiger. Their clowns were amateur, and the jugglers and acrobats were teenagers selected from the high school athletics teams.

Needing direction and facing bankruptcy after years of receiving only half in ticket sales and earnings, the Barnes circus quickly declined. In desperation, Barnes signed on with Bigham to receive an average weekly salary from total ticket sales.

Preferring animals over acrobats, Barnes assisted Barnham by trading rings with him between acts and promenades.

Barnes' voice was naturally soft—Tenor.

The 'Sengerphone,' one identical to Barham's, also served as a dependable aid to him.

Through the use of the voice magnifier apparatus and from years of practice of telling compelling stories, Henry Barnes' melodious and kind delivery benefitted by gaining a more boisterous presence in the ring.

Example: "OK, Boys and Girls! Are you ready to be dazzled by some of the most amazingly talented puppies you've ever witnessed? Are you?? Well then, here they are! Let us all rattle the tent with shouts of delight and the clapping of hands for the inimitable "Pappy's Peppy," singsonging the last syllable while fading off at the end, "Puppieeeeeeeeeeeeeeeeeeeeeeeeees!!!!"

Then, Barnes would retreat from the ring to stalls holding six full-grown African elephants, directing their line-up and entrance for the finale promenade.

On a typical day, Bigham made certain the clowns received all the timely cues for their free-spirited exaggerations beneath the main tent.

Now, by being his principal partner, Julius also claimed ownership of a particular object.

This object was something Barnes owned but had never used himself. He had, in fact, inherited it as it was; A large, heavy, folded and tightly wrapped circus tent looking ordinary as it sat.

On Jeremy's first birthday, Julius had the tent unwrapped and lifted.

It outwardly appeared benign and harmless, but both partners were acutely aware of the unexplainable mystery contained within its risen space.

Gramps

The old clown wasn't one inclined toward verbose conversation. When asked about his experience prior to the circus, he would simply smile or nod.

Sometimes he'd aim a trick gun at your face while emitting a maniacal laugh. Upon the pulling of the trigger, the result would be the dropping of a silk banner with the word 'BANG!' printed upon it.

Everyone there learned very quickly that when that banner fell, the normal conversation would abruptly end with a communal laugh.

Jeremy had been repeatedly warned by his father to stay away from the clown tent and the clowns, but the clown tent was like another home to him.

Taking special interest in Jeremy's propensity, Gramps never discouraged him from coming around to visit inside the clown tent.

He wanted Jeremy to experience for himself what it is like being in their presence.

Being aware of Jeremy's father's directives for avoidance, Gramps negated this by stating that he could "Deal directly with the 'Old Man'" and continued his open invitation for Jeremy's casual visit.

But, Gramps was not well. That day before matinee, Jeremy walked up to the clown tent to inquire about Gramps' medical condition, finding still a very ill report.

"Why don't you send a wire to the new upstart, Lou Jacobs? We could use another ringer," asked Julius.

"But, Julius, we already have Dynamo," replied Barnes.

"He can do just about anything. No one dares trying to upstage him! Besides, Lou is with John's bunch, you know that."

Lou Jacobs was just starting out as a multi-talented circus clown.

His usual dress was a checkered-pink-on striped lavender suit coat, baggy pants with a 12-inch-high collar, big shoes and a small umbrella attached to a 10-foot handle.

Later in life, he would become credited for inventing the 'Clown Car,' a motorized mini-vehicle which could contain thirteen clowns and seven dogs without reservation.

"Besides, the season is coming mid. We can't change the routine now," said Barnes.

On a fair-weathered Sunday morning, the circus was preparing for the first in an afternoon of three one-hour matinee performances starting after early church service, 11:00am and ending at 3:30 PM.

That morning before church, an incident took place around the Bigham family breakfast table involving Jeremy, his sister and ultimately, his father.

This would involve a children's book but would affect Jeremy's life beyond his wildest expectations.

Thaddeus Barnes

Henry Barnes' great-uncle, Thaddeus, the founder of, 'Barnes' Bonanza Circus,' was also a part-time writer, keeping journals of everyday circus life and compiling them into an obscure but published children's book. It was a book reflecting his personal love for the circus, with focus on the clowns and on an elusive world which might exist somewhere between here and there; A place unseen, but not very far away: 'Clown World.'

In the book, Clown World is described as a place where everyone and everything is physically and environmentally exaggerated.

All animals, insects and other living beings are clown-like in both appearance and behavior.

Henry had loaned the book to Jeremy.

Jeremy took to the book as a fly takes to honey.

When his mother called him in for breakfast, he barely had enough time to close it on the chapter where the main character actually sets journey into the Abyss.

Deciding he could hide the pages among his sermon notes and continue to read while holding it low beneath the table, that's just what he did, hoping the family would think he was reading his Bible, preparing for Sunday school lesson.

It was while doing so when his father noticed he wasn't actively eating.

"Jeremy. Eat your breakfast. We mustn't be late for morning services," demanded Father.

There was a momentary pause.

"Big day! Three matinees!" continued Julius.

Jeremy never looked up.

Father noticed his son's lazy attention. This time, scoldingly.

"Jeremy, your breakfast is getting cold! You must not be wasteful with food. Now, eat!"

Kate, Jeremy's sister, has already been described, and it was at this very moment when her reputation became chiseled in stone.

After being up from the table to fetch more hot biscuits from the oven, she couldn't help but notice her brother's covert demeanor, one she herself recognized through practiced experience.

"What are you reading?" she asked. "Anything interesting?"

She snatches the book from Jeremy's possession and proceeds to read the cover.

"Clown World. Hmmm. How does this have anything to do with church?"

"Let me have it!" pleaded Jeremy.

"Give that to me!"

Father sounded serious.

He looked at the cover, then the back, quickly flipped through a few pages, and then paused.

A wrinkle of disapproval slowly replaced an expressionless forehead.

"Where did you get this?" demanded Father.

"Mr. Barnes loaned it to me before breakfast. He said his great-uncle wrote it," replied Jeremy.

"Rubbish!" shouted Father, turning around to the fireplace behind him and throwing the book face up onto well-established cinders.

There, its back and edges slowly blackened in the coals, becoming curled and finally indiscernible.

"Jeremy, stay away from the clowns. Do you understand me? Stay away from the clowns!"

'Yes, Father," replied Jeremy. "I understand."

This was going to be a hard promise to keep.

Jeremy had been repeatedly warned by his father to keep his distance from the clown tent and the clowns.

The clown tent was like another home to him. It was a place where everyone knew his name.

After the family arose from the table, Jeremy returned to the fireplace, retrieving whatever was left of the book. Luckily, only the covers were damaged.

Jeremy took it, ran back to his room, and continued to read it several times over, knowing not how to explain its present condition to Mr. Barnes when the time came to return it.

Damaged or not, its purpose had been well-utilized.

The Inhabitants

In the book, all people here, whom we shall forthrightly refer to as 'Real Clowns,' possess the following physical attributes:

Exceptionally large feet, highly arched eyebrows upon the face making room for protruding eyelashes.

Crimson bottom lips, noses, navels, nipples upon the breasts and buttocks--All of these appearing otherwise normal, not unlike our own, just deeply red.

Exaggerated head circumferences, with children measuring as little as five inches around and adults as much as twenty-five. Some heads would be long and thin, while others, big and round.

Today, a person completely bald sans a single, solitary living hair follicle from the center, might tomorrow pride in locks of tangled frizz surrounding a shiny-clean dome.

A clinical disorder common among these inhabitants could be described in the opposite of coulrophobia,' a fear of clowns. Rather, 'anthropophobia,' a fear of people.

Also, one must realize that a clown's fits could cause one to go berserk, such as jumping head first out a window or pulling out the hair by the roots.

First Matinee

Julius, who was already busy herding animals in for the promenade, was there, standing with Mr. Barnes.

"Ok, ok, let's go! Hurry! Everyone! You've fifteen seconds to get to your places! Come on! What do you think this is, a picnic? Hey! Get that elephant from the stall, now! Gramps! Gramps! Get your clowns out here, and Pronto!"

With some important business to discuss, Barnes attempted, and Jeremy too, unsuccessfully, to obtain Julius' undivided attention, who seemed too busy to discuss anything of importance at that moment in time.

"Father. Father, I must speak with you," begged Jeremy.

"Not now, Son," Julius retorted.

"But, Father! I must…"

Barnes intervened.

"Not now, Jeremy. Your father is presently busy."

Barnes turned to Bigham.

"Full house."

Bigham dryly replied, "Yeah."

"What's with Gramps?" inquired Barnes.

"I don't know, Henry. He's getting old. We're all getting old," replied Julius.

Cautiously, Barnes attempted to open a conversation with Bigham, again.

"Julius, I know this isn't exactly the appropriate time to talk about this but…"

Barnes is interrupted.

"What's the matter with you? Have you sawdust in your panties? Get those riggers out here before the sun sets on your absent-minded insolence!"

"Jeremy," said Barnes to the boy.

"Your father is pre-occupied. Let me take you down to the midway for some cotton candy. Maybe a hot dog?" "I'm not hungry," replied Jeremy.

"Very well, then", answered Barnes.

In applicable note: In the year 1930, the Mars candy company invented the first 'Snickers' bar. They were sold for 5 cents a bar.

Barnes had become addicted to them, usually carrying two or three in his inside and outside coat pockets.

Barnes reached into one of his pockets, pulling out a wrapped candy and handing it to Jeremy.

"Here. You might want this later," said Barnes along with a gentle wink.

Jeremy put the Snickers in his vest pocket, where it was sticking out, just a little, alongside his treasured harmonica.

Pausing for a moment, Jeremy said, "Thank you," before running straight back to the clown tent, where there already was much activity.

On his way, Jeremy made sure he wasn't to be seen entering the clown tent, and once there, he lingered close around the side where he could peer in through a hole in the canvas wall.

Through the hole, he observed Gramps lying down in a bed made of hay as a makeshift mattress and a horse blanket as cover for warmth. A pony saddle served as his pillow, and a pair of his own worn-out, flannel pajamas had been wrapped around the saddle, creating a soft cushion for Gramps' tired old head.

Giggles, one of the troupes, was near, serving

Gramps small sips of straight gin from a weathered tin cup.

Since he was only just a few yards away, Jeremy could plainly interpret most of their audible conversation.

Giggles spoke with his distinctive Irish accent.

"Come on, Gramps. You can do it. Take a little sip. Just a little. That's it. Good..."

Gramps took a sip, then coughed.

There were worried clowns all around. Not a lot of talking could be heard, except for uncharacteristic whispers under exuberant Sousa marches coming from the bandstand.

The music accompanied wire walkers, who were crossing a 100 ft. high wire on unicycles, juggling cabbages, heads of lettuce and small melons.

Another high-wire act consisted of a trained poodle peddling a doggiesized unicycle.

The first of many clown cues, this one involved a camel who refuses to stand up and walk properly before finally being mounted. A frantic gallop ensued with a clumsy rider in precarious tow.

"Giggles. Do me a favor, will you?" asked Gramps.

"Tell Jeremy to bring me my medicine. It's in the footlocker beside my bunk."

"But, Gramps, you know that Jeremy isn't allowed in the clown tent. The old man would have a fit. I'll get it for you."

"No. You bring Jeremy. I'll deal with the old man," said Gramps.

Jeremy had been all the while listening closely to this conversation. He suddenly emerged from hiding.

"I'm right here, Gramps."

"Jeremy, my boy! I knew you'd come around here. Can't keep you away from the real fun, can we?" (Coughs).

"Gramps, I'll get your medicine," said Jeremy.

"No. Come close. I want to tell you something."

Jeremy drew close to Gramps, whose voice is now very weak and thin.

"Sometimes a man has to make tough decisions about what he's going to do with his life...how he's going to make his mark in the world. Are you listening, Son?"

"Yes, Gramps. I'm listening."

"You hang on to it."

"Hang on to what?" Jeremy asked.

"The child."

'What child? What are you talking about, Gramps?"

"The child...that's right there...deep in your heart...deep in your mind...Don't let him go. Promise me you'll do that, Son."

"Yes, Gramps. I will. I promise."

"That's good. That's very good."

Gramps continued to struggle with a raspy cough before Giggles once again intervened.

"Hurry, Boy. Get his medicine!"

Jeremy started out running through the carnival to the clown bunkhouse. Upon arrival, he took the medicine stored in Gramps' footlocker.

Urgently, he started running back before meeting the formidable figure of his father standing before him.

"Jeremy, where's your mother?" asked Julius.

"I, um...I think she went to collect on the midway," said Jeremy.

"Very well. If you see her, tell her to come back right away. We'll go to dinner."

'Yes, Father."

Bigham walked away.

Jeremy waited only a split moment before he turned to run back to the clown tent.

He is too late with the medicine, however, for Gramps had already died.

"Here's your medicine…Gramps." Reality took precedence.

"Gramps! Gramps!!!" cried Jeremy.

Dynamo walked up to find Jeremy in tears of extreme mourning.

"Oh, Dynamo! I couldn't run back fast enough! It's my fault!"

"No, Son, it is not your fault! Gramps was ready to go. He gave all he had in him...right up to the end. He was very, very tired. Now, he's at peace with the Universe. With himself."

Jeremy looked down at the medicine bottle he still held in his hand as Dynamo slowly took it from him.

Jeremy asked, "What happens now...with the clowns?"

Noodles was one of the few female members of the troupe.

"Jeremy," she said, "Gramps saw something very special in you. He had a real knack for recognizing the specialness in people!"

In unison, the others agreed.

"Yes! Yes!"

Noodles continued.

"And you, Jeremy Bigham…You are a very, very special boy!"

A familiar voice aided by the Sengerphone boomed above all the cacophony.

"TO YOUR PLACES!"

Dynamo whispered to Giggles.

"I can't leave right now. Somebody oughta go and tell the old man that Gramps is gone."

Dynamo looked squarely into Giggles' painted eyes as she nodded in affirmation and scurried off.

Dynamo then took Jeremy aside, walking while talking.

"You really love the clowns, don't you, Son?"

"I sure do, Dynamo. I sure do."

"You want to be one of us, don't you, Son?"

"Yes! I do! More than anything! But, Father...he won't allow..."

Dynamo suddenly gained a coy look about him, one that Jeremy had never seen in him before.

"Don't you worry about your father or your mother. They don't really understand you like Gramps did...like all of us do. Come with me."

Otto, a character portrait of a slight autistic, spoke.

"Dynamo! Are you sure you want to do

this?" "I'm sure, Otto. I have to. It's

tradition, you know."

Otto nodded.

Dynamo put his arm around Jeremy's shoulder, continuing to walk and talk together while making his way toward an unused corner of the tent.

The band could be heard playing a lilting musical arrangement of "Laugh, Clown, Laugh."

Dynamo spoke.

"You know, before I joined your Father's circus, I could have taken a job as an accountant. I would have had my own office and everything. I could have spent years and years doing the same old thing. Working...coming home...sleeping...getting up again to work."

"I was sure that along the way, I would forget how to smile...how to laugh. So, I made a tough decision by turning down that offer and instead, became a full-time circus clown. From that moment on, everything has remained right in my life--everything. I already knew that while I was making other people smile, I would also be smiling myself. It felt good. I kept re-discovering the child in me."

"Just like Gramps said."

"That's right, Jeremy. Gramps knew all about it."

"Jeremy, if you really want to be a clown, we'll help you!"

"Really? Oh, Dynamo, I really want to be a clown."

"You're sure, right?"

"Yes, I'm sure. Very sure."

"Alright. Alright! Everyone. Jeremy wants to be a clown. A real clown." Everyone cheered.

"There's only one way of becoming a real clown, Jeremy. You must learn to live it."

"But, before you proceed, my boy, you must hurry and choose a new name for yourself - a clown name. Hurry, because we don't have that much time."

Jeremy said, "But, Dynamo, I can't think of a name so quickly."

Dynamo paused.

"Okay, but remember that from this moment onwards, you are no longer Jeremy Bigham. You are whomever you decide to be, inside and out, according to your chosen clown name."

Dynamo handed Jeremy a standard costume clown nose.

"Here. Put this on. You don't want to scare anyone."

As Jeremy donned the nose, Dynamo noticed the Snickers bar that Mr. Barnes had given to him.

After giving Jeremy's nose a small, approving adjustment, he says to him,

"Snickers…"

"What?" Jeremy retorted.

"I know," said Dynamo. "It's the name of a candy bar, but it'll be good for now."

"Perfect fit! It's your time, boy. Now, go and get it!"

Dynamo reached down to a corner of the tent and lifts a hidden canvas flap.

There, revealed a portal leading directly into the Clown World.

Jeremy steps through.

He is observed leaving through the portal just before his father comes into the clown tent.

Bigham walked in. "Where did you put him?"

"He's in his bunk," answered Otto.

"I called the coroner. He'll be here any minute. Don't make a scene. We don't want to scare away the paying customers, right?"

"Right, Mr. Bigham," said Otto.

"Dynamo, have you seen Jeremy?"

"Who? Jeremy? Why, no, we haven't seen him, have we?"

"No, no…" said the others.

"Well, if you do, tell him to come home right away after the matinee."

"Yes, sir." He looked at Dynamo.

"Dynamo, what are you doing?" asked Otto.

Dynamo, being goofily hostile, replies, "Who is in charge of the clowns now, Otto? Is it me?"

"Dynamo! You and Gramps were always just like brothers to each other. You know more about running a circus, more than anyone I know... because you're a real clown!"

Dynamo came close to Otto and whispered, "That's right. My nose won't wash off, like yours!"

Dynamo grabs Otto's nose, which is attached with an elastic band around his head, pulls it straight out and lets it go. Dynamo laughs hysterically.

"Hee-hee-hee-hee-hee-hee-hee-hee! Heee!"

"I'm going back for a while. You are in charge of the clowns now, Otto!"

"Wait a minute, Dynamo! You can't just leave us here! Who is going to do the second and third matinees?"

"You take over for me, Otto. You've seen my act a million times."

"I can't do what you do!" Otto said in anguish.

"Sure you can! You just have to sing a couple of songs and tell a few jokes while juggling on a unicycle. What's so hard about that, Otto?"

"Dynamo, are you kidding me? I just run around blowing a siren whistle while sprinkling the audience with confetti. I can't sing and I don't know how to juggle or ride a unicycle."

"You'll be fine." saying so, Dynamo walked away.

"But Dynamo! Dynamo! Wait a minute...!"

"See you later!"

Otto shook his head. "The old man is going to kill us!"

Dynamo also passed through the portal leading into Clown World.

Sounds of crying could be heard throughout the clown tent while the coroner was in the bunkhouse, covering Gramps' body with a sheet. Silently, he got lifted onto a cot then loaded into a waiting, unmarked wagon.

Everyone turned slowly toward the portal.

Chapter Two

One might think that moving from one universe to another would involve sounds, disorienting wormholes and flashing colors, but this wasn't the case. It was more like moving between two conjoined bubbles having a liquid center allowing free but precarious, passage through.

At once, Jeremy found himself standing at a dead end of an alley. There was still enough daylight to see clearly to the end of the alley.

Jeremy turned around to look for the portal from where he just came, but it had disappeared into a solid brick wall with an occasional weathered, advertising billboard.

As fingers ran along brick and mortar, the young mind suddenly considered that he had not inquired as to how to return from Clown World once he was there.

A chill of worry travelled through Jeremy's being as he turned to face four individuals standing about 25 yards away.

Jeremy's first impulse was to smile and greet, but instead, he remained still and silent. One of the individuals came a little closer and said,

"Oh! What do we have here? You're a formal, right? Well, you sure ain't a hobo! What's your name?"

Jeremy remained silent.

The person speaking to him was male, about 200 pounds, 5'4" tall, orange hair, tattered top hat and clothing, smoking a huge cigar which continuously changed corners of his mouth as he spoke.

The other three individuals were also male.

One was tall and lanky and wore a baseball cap sideways.

Another was short, bald and had a large white rat with a red nose sitting on his head.

The other looked to be 99 years old and was clothed in a whisky barrel.

They peered at Jeremy while coming closer and asking more questions.

The tall one asked, "Where did you come from, boy?"

"There ain't been nobody out here at this end, 'cept us. Ain't that right, boys?"

"Yeah, yeah, that's right. Yep, yep, yep."

"Ain't cha got a tongue? Can you talk? Ha!"

"Maybe he's a mime! That's it! He's a Formal Mime. That's what you are, ain't it? Huh?"

A long pause ensued.

"Well, say somethin'! What's your name? What is it?"

Jeremy decided it was time for him to find a way out of the alley. He reached for his harmonica, but instead pulled out the Snickers bar Mr. Barnes had given him.

"Snickers! That's it! I'm Snickers the Clown!"

Jeremy traded the candy for the harmonica in his pocket and began to sing and play:

"Who is the clown that's all over the town?

It's Snickers the Clown, that's me!

Who is the clown where the music abounds?

It's Snickers the Clown, that's me"

"You'll never meet a clown more thrilling,

I'll bring the house down, there's none more willing,

And before I go, I want you to know,

I'm Snickers the Clown…There's none more thrilling.

I'm Snickers the Clown…There's none more willing."

At this point in the song, Jeremy managed to make his way onto their turf, singing, dancing and playing the harmonica. By this time, all the alley clowns had really gotten into the music. The verse ended and Jeremy yelled,

"Now everyone, sing along!"

They did just that, getting into the music long enough for Jeremy to run into the daylight and open spaces.

The sound of the harmonica could be heard doing a gradual diminuendo.

The alley clowns barely noticed until the harmonica could no longer be heard.

"Hey! Where'd he go?" said one.

"Let's follow him."

"Yeah! We'll see where he hangs out! Come on."

Jeremy had gotten a good head start as he ran across what appeared to be a park. There, he paused to get his breath long enough for him to spot his alley clown friends emerging from their lair, coming in his direction.

Jeremy continued to run through a golf course where he observed players golfing with shovels, hitting beach balls down a course completely covered in holes.

Unlike our game, the idea here was to keep the ball from falling into a hole.

One would holler, "Four!" while four beach balls would fall into the Swiss cheese-like course.

Another might swing causing the ball to go straight up into the air, high above the player's head.

A player might frantically swing at nothing before he finally hits the ball. It flies and becomes captured into one of many holes, surprising a sewer worker or a disgruntled rodent.

Forthrightly, one of the alley clowns spotted Jeremy.

"There he is!"

They started running toward the park.

Jeremy did not know that he had been spotted, so he was now not running, but walking around to the front of the golf course clubhouse.

There, he saw a purple and yellow limousine containing a pair of exuberantly inebriated individuals, dressed in appropriately flamboyant golf attire, obviously out for a good time.

Another could be seen telescopically compacting each of his golf clubs, putting them into his pocket, followed by the folding of a golf cart as one would a napkin, placing it into a briefcase and walking away.

There was a small person leading a lizard on leash.

Watching an individual buy a shirt from the pro shop, Jeremy learned that in this world, the idea is to not be in possession of any currency.

The provider would pay the customer upon purchase for whatever the price it was to receive the service or product.

Example: A person might choose one-hundred dollars in groceries.

The store from which they were purchased, exchanges the merchandise plus one-hundred-dollars in currency.

Clown money is reminiscent of our old-fashioned, toy, 'Play Money', except these have a picture of a, 'Jack-in-the-Box', on the front and a circus tent on the back.

People were constantly receiving money and then quickly getting rid of it.

It was those ending up with the most stuff and the least countable money who win in this economy.

Upon learning this odd practice, Jeremy remembered a buffalo nickel he'd been saving for quite some time.

When he spotted a soft-drink machine, he reached under his stocking and extracted the nickel, assuming he'd get it back once it was spent.

So, Jeremy put in his nickel, chose a drink, 'Kooky Kola', and sure enough, a nickel came back in change along with his drink.

Happily, he returned the coin back to his sock before taking a long, satisfying sip.

He had no sooner swallowed when the orange-haired alley clown suddenly appeared before him.

"There you are… Snickers, huh?! You could make us a lot of dough and
I don't mean money. I mean dough. Cookie dough. We love cookies!"

Jeremy began to speak when a hand grabbed him by the arm, pulling him in rapid, zig-zag directions until his observers fell into a state of confusion.

Before they could make a target of him, Jeremy had darted off into another, unknown direction.

Jeremy's abductor continued this guiding.

 A female voice said, "Hurry up! Do not tally here! Come with

me!" Jeremy was being pulled along for what seemed

like miles.

Along the way, as in scenes from some crazy animation, Jeremy observed the activities:

Male and female executives going to work clutching brightly colored briefcases, striding the sidewalks carrying tiny umbrellas and carpooling into parking lots into very compact automobiles.

Utility workers, perched upon tall unicycles, traversing along unstable power lines.

Two babies were in a crib. One sucks upon an oversized bottle while the other enjoys a five-decker, multi-flavored ice cream cone.

The baby with the cream snatches the bottle from the others' mouth while the sibling begins to cry floods of tears from its pores. The victimized baby then snatches the cone from the others' hand, skillfully depositing it squarely upon the nose of the twin. It too begins to cry resulting in a stream of tears to flow down the street as does a river from a sudden cloudburst.

A man with a cold, sneezed while confetti flew from his nose.

A family partakes in a picnic together. Parents were conversing while a sister shot her brother out of a cannon.

At a pond, a man caught a fish with a red nose and lips.

Along a school running track, athletic racers began from start positions.

As they ran, one could hear the flop, flop, flopping of huge, flat feet. Generally, an apparent winner is disqualified because of one foot being well over the starting line.

In front of a neighborhood tavern, individuals were

sitting around, getting very high from sucking on balloon pipe animals and passing them.

At one point, Jeremy's yet-unidentified captor ducked momentarily into a men's public restroom.

There, while taking care of his much needed natural business, Jeremy observed four clown shoes under one, closed door stall.

One of the pairs of shoes were not touching the floor.

Jeremy chose his own stall beside them.

There, he overheard a father assisting his son who was struggling with a painfully, constipated bowel.

The father said to the child,

"Here. Let me help."

What resulted was a bouquet of flowers being extracted, resulting in the youngster's immediate relief.

As soon as Jeremy emerged from the restroom, the rescuing hand grabbed him once again and they continued with the maniacal expedition through the town.

In a bakery, a chef could be seen through the storefront window, baking a cake.

The ingredients of flour, milk and eggs were being poured into a man's hat and placed into a hot oven.

Within a matter of seconds, a fully baked cake was taken out, complete with frosting and burning candles.

Perhaps, the most curious of locations, at least to Jeremy, was a church.

It had a cross adorning its transom.

Music emerged from the inside and wafted into the busy streets, so it was assumed a religious service was in progress.

Not his father, but his mother had instilled into him a sense of belonging to a congregation who supported concepts of charity and love, repentance and salvation.

Spirituality was a subject of interest rivaled only by Jeremy's keen fascination with the clowns.

So, Jeremy stayed for a while, pondering the sound of the calliope, playing hymns executed in a comic, unusually jovial, harmonic style.

The, 'um-pah, um-pah', reminded him of how bands would render their marches and novelty arrangements for the circus.

His mind had wandered. He momentarily forgot the dangers privy to his trail.

Precisely then, the aggressors spotted him again.

The hand with the yet-unseen face continued to pull him along.

The hand was quick and Jeremy was sweating and out of breath.

A clever maneuver of hiding behind a newsstand saved him from discovery as the aggressors passed in haste, then completely out of sight.

Penelope and Mergetroid

This had been a seemingly long journey from the time Jeremy had passed through the tent portal to this place of quiet sanctuary… a small, modest dwelling with a living room area not unlike his own in Baraboo.

Jeremy scanned the room to view photos of family, trophies and knickknacks.

On a prominent wall hung a classic portrait of Christ with His right hand up.

He sported a red nose and lips.

Jeremy's female abductor eluded his full view, but she spoke again, only this time in complete sentence.

"You must be very hungry from your long journey here. How about something sweet to eat? I just made this banana cream pie. I was going to throw it at someone, like my husband, Mergetroid, because today is a special occasion. Here! There's plenty! Eat up!"

The woman, without turning to face him, handed Jeremy the pie along with a large, wooden spoon.

Jeremy took the pie from the hand and began to taste. It was very sweet and equally delicious.

"I am Penelope. What is your name?"

"Jeremy. I am Jeremy."

"Jeremy. Jeremy. Who gave you that name? It reveals nothing about you. We'll come up with a better name for you."

She continued to evade Jeremy's full view.

Jeremy continued to eat and nearly finished before

she said,

"Hey! You have whipped cream on your nose!"

Upon this alert, Jeremy looked up long enough to see his protector's face, which was too close to gain adequate focus.

All he could see was a red nose nearly touching his own, costume nose. She silently signaled with a finger to her nose that there was something on his.

Jeremy began to dig into his vest pockets in search of a tissue.

He felt his harmonica, then found the forgotten Snickers bar that Mr. Barnes had given to him earlier that morning.

Jeremy removed it from his pocket and read the wrapper out loud.

"Snickers."

 "Snickers?" Penelope inquired with a surprised lilt.

"My name can be Snickers", said Jeremy.

With a chuckle, Penelope retorts,

"That sounds more like a name for a dog, but I suppose it will do for now."

Jeremy began to laugh and Penelope laughed right along with him. Their laughter got more and more hysterical and then subsided into a serious mode of reality.

As they calmed, the two finally paused to consider a frontal view of each other from foot to face, as would a camera in an impressionistic film.

Penelope

She was gentle in appearance.

Her shoes were large, but conservative. Her dress was long and flowing with a subdued daisy pattern and soft color. There were ruffles here and there, especially around the ankles and wrists.

Her face was lightly transparent with white face, with a distinctive normal nose, very red but not characteristically bulbous - more natural in shape than expected.

She possessed a sweet smile with gently painted lips and high eyebrows, as is distinctive in this genus.

Jeremy felt very comfortable in her presence.

"Where did you get those clothes?" she asked.

"You can't go out into the world dressed like that. For Heaven's sake!"

"Heaven…" said the boy, without inflection but with an implication of interest.

"What about Heaven?" she replied.

Jeremy continued, "Are there clowns there… in Heaven?"

The sound of the calliope could still be heard from this space.

"What a silly question! You know the answer to that, Snickers. Here, try this on."

Penelope handed Jeremy a shirt, pants, shoes and an extended tube of red lipstick. She proceeds to paint his nose with it.

"And always wear this nose, wherever you go. Without it, you would be naked."

She continued to gently paint Jeremy's nose so that no natural skin color would cause holiday.

"And I have more news for you," as she came closer and whispered.

"Our noses aren't the only things that are red, if you know what I mean".

"No, I really don't!" he replied.

Her whispers became more private:

"Remove all your clothes and you'd also be removing all doubt."

She winked.

"Now, lift your shirt."

'What?!" Jeremy winced at the thought, startled even more that a clown would ask him to do such a thing, especially a female one.

"Lift my shirt? Why?"

"You'll see."

Penelope took the tube of lipstick, advanced the product to its limit and proceeded to paint Jeremy's nipples with a bright, regal red, the same color as his nose.

"Hey! That tickles!"

Penelope moved to Jeremy's navel.

"There, too? You've got to be

kidding!" "There! You can put your

shirt down now," said Penelope.

Jeremy did as she instructed.

"We don't have time to paint your butt right now."

"What? My butt?!"

As could be imagined, Jeremy was completely flabbergasted.

"It seems to me that maybe, you've done this kind of thing before," wondered Jeremy.

"Well, yes," said Penelope.

"We had a visitor once, a long time ago, with about the same age and looks about him as you, but he wasn't anything like you. He was very different. Different, indeed."

"What was different about them?" asked Jeremy.

"Oh, that's an easy question. This boy didn't have it in him."

"He didn't have what in him?" Jeremy inquired.

She laughs dryly, without smiling.

"'The Child' He didn't have 'The Child' in his mind or in his heart. That was the difference. Now ask me a harder question."

Jeremy was paralyzed in thought concerning this last conversation.

"What's the matter, boy? You look like a kid with another question.
Come on. Ask me."

"How… how did you know? How could you tell?" asked Jeremy.

"Tutt, tutt. It's obvious! Even a simple court jester could discern that! You're the genuine article, no doubt!"

She paused.

"Do I look stupid to you? I think not! Duh, duh, duh!"

"Now change out of those nasty clothes. You should look presentable for my husband, Mergetroid."

An expression of endearment overtook her.

"He's a good man. We've been married for

37 years."

She looked away in sadness.

"We never could have children of our own. He's contracted a condition", she said.

"He was a singing juggler. A tenor. One day, an accident occurred."

'What happened? May I ask?"

"Certainly," she assured.

"One of his balls hit the ground, bounced up and knocked out all but one of his front teeth. He just mumbles now, more soprano than before. He goes to work every morning, comes home to eat and in the evening, does his 'clownly' activities."

"Where does he work? Does he still juggle?" asked Jeremy.

"Oh, yes! He is a fine juggler. He works at the shipyard's juggling cargo. He's been there for 42 years, tomorrow. Today is our wedding anniversary," she replied.

"Wow!", exclaimed Jeremy. "Congratulations! How, where did you meet?"

"We met on line," answered Penelope.

"On line? Where is on line?" asked Jeremy.

"On line... at the grocery store," she replied.

"He was buying crackers and sardines for lunch and for some reason, he offered to share them with me. He had all his teeth then. And, all his hair! Ha! Ha!"

The precarious sounds of a sputtering, gasoline engine could be heard outside the residence.

"Oh! There he is! Hurry now and get yourself dressed!"

Jeremy left the living room carrying his new clothes with him.

Mergetroid

A vehicle with multiple mechanical issues had just pulled into the driveway.

The car's radio was on, playing a Doctor Laura-type program, discussing a serious, clown-ly topic.

The car continued to shake, sputter and backfire long minutes after the engine was disengaged. Finally, an explosive percussion preceded a shower of colorful confetti from the chariot's exhaust.

In the driver's seat was a man known to everyone as Mergetroid.

He prepared himself to meet his wife on the occasion of their wedding anniversary.

He was thin in build, with a tall, narrow head.

He was humming an unrecognizable melody in a soprano voice of lessthan-accurate pitch.

He primped, looking into a tiny mirror, pulling renegade nose, hairs with a pair of pliers.

He was wearing a hat with no middle.

From its crown, there stood one solitary, foot-long hair, not requiring removal of the hat to brush straight up. He did this with great care for perched upon the hair's pinnacle was a worm.

The worm was also wearing a hat identical to his.

It was humming the same tune while brushing its one hair.

He turned off the radio and before exiting the car, he remembered that he had brought a bouquet of fresh daisies for his bride.

As he stood to walk to his door, the worm jumped from his hair to rest upon one of the flower's green leaves.

As he walked up to the front door of his home, he paused, straightened his posture and from his hat, produced a nose flute.

He rang the doorbell and began to play with his nose the tune, 'I Love You Truly'.

Penelope came to answer the door, while fluttering her eyelashes in her husband's direction.

As the song approached the bridge, Penelope took in a long sniff of the flower's sweet aroma. As she did, the worm hung tightly onto the leaf so that it was not sucked up into her large nostrils. As the song concluded, she sneezed and the worm held tightly to the leaf to keep from being blown away by her windy exhale.

Mergetroid addressed his bride.

"(Mumble), These, (mumble), are for, (mumble), you, (mumble, mumble, mumble)," as he handed the bouquet to Penelope.

"Oh, Mergetroid! You shouldn't have. They're just beautiful. Thank you!" said Penelope.

"(Mumbles), Oooouuuhhhh, ummm ummm, oh, hee hee!"

Penelope giggled.

They entered the house together, clutching arms while Penelope tightly held her daisies.

"I have a surprise for you, too, Sweetheart! Snickers? Snickers come out and meet my husband, Mergetroid."

Jeremy walked slowly from the bedroom dressed in his new clown wardrobe. He stood there motionless while Penelope formally introduced them.

"It is my pleasure to meet you, sir," said Jeremy, reaching out as a gentleman to cordially shake Mergetriod's hand.

"Mumble, mumble, mumble," answered Mergetroid.

 Penelope interpreted,

"He says it's a pleasure to meet such a polite little man."

Thank you, Sir," said Jeremy.

"Mumble, mumble, mumble, mumble."

Penelope continued to interpret,

"He said you don't have to call him 'Sir'. All his friends call him, Mergetroid."

Jeremy smiled.

"Okay, Mergetroid!"

"Snickers has come to stay with us for a little while. Do you mind?"

"Oh, I don't want to be of any trouble to you," says Jeremy.

"Mumble, mumble, mumble."

"You're absolutely right! There's no curmudgeon in him. Not like the last one," says Penelope.

"Why don't you wash up for dinner, Dear, while Snickers and I get ready in the kitchen. Come on, Snickers."

Penelope follows Jeremy into the kitchen.

She still has the daisies in her clutch and stops momentarily at the kitchen door to look down at her flowers and look back adoringly toward her groom.

She throws him a kiss while the worm hides his eyes, but takes a sneak peek at them from beneath the brim of its hat.

Not taking her fluttering eyes off of him, Penelope backs slowly into the kitchen.

Mergetroid also backs his way into the bedroom, dancing and singing:

"I think I'm gonna get me some, (mumble, mumble), "get me some", (mumble, mumble).

The worm sings and dances, too.

Jeremy Matures

Years had passed. Now, Jeremy was in young adolescent prime.

His body was proportionate as an average boy of his age, fourteen, but more firm and stout than before.

Course hair was beginning to appear on his chin, making it apparent that a sharp razor may soon be of necessary employ.

There was also an awakening of self-efficacy, where the confident Jeremy once dwelled, now more so the persona of, 'Snickers the Clown'.

His wardrobe, although still finely tailored, reflected a new spirit of color and design.

Now, he sported a cap not unlike that of a sailor. His vest and coat with tail resembled those worn by English horsemen. His trousers were bilious upon the leg and his shoes, although large, were wing-tipped.

There was very little recollection of his former life as Jeremy Bigham, son of Julius.

What developed was mostly psychological, thoughts spurred by a strict upbringing dominated by less-than-personable, parental guidance.

His surrogate parents, Penelope and Mergetroid, were the antithesis from his natural-born origin.

Now, from his being amongst the real clowns of this world, it would become necessary to exercise capricious shenanigan and innocent tomfoolery in his every day life.

New skills accompanied ordinary habit as 'Snickers' was emerging as a adept musician, singer and dancer.

His harmonica prowess had greatly matured, becoming more technical and articulate.

A widened repertoire of song enhanced the image of poet and troubadour.

His songs possessed a new manner of reveal, portraying complex emotions within simple rhyme.

As he grew, interests concerning matters of the heart and soul took precedence.

In school, a formidable interest toward the opposite sex replaced a previously juvenile indifference.

One classmate in particular received his primary focus.

Puddin, a daughter of middle-classed-parents with eyes of blue, hair of green and with delicate voice.

Puddin's attention toward Jeremy was not to be ignored.

She would find opportunity to linger close to him whenever possible.

It had become daily practice for the two youngsters to walk together to and from school and it was not uncommon for them to share class notes or to study together before class.

One day as they made their way home, something occurred, making Jeremy tremble in his shoes...very large shoes.

A bus full of students stopped at a crossing.

Peering out the window was a girl who appeared slightly older than both Jeremy or Puddin.

Her resemblance to sister Kate was uncanny, only she had clown attributes.

This was an indication that in this world, everyone had a counterpart...a 'doppelgänger or an exact copy of the original person.

From this time forward, this awareness overcame the lad.

"What's the matter, Snickers?," asked Puddin. "You look like you've seen a ghost!"

"Perhaps I have," answered Snickers.

"It's nothing. Let's go."

Intuitions were correct, for in this parallel world, everything had a counterpart, something which Jeremy had not considered before.

His family and friends might all exist here.

His primary fear was that he might encounter his own double.

A Cottage Affair

Falls preceded Winters and Springs passed into Summers. By this time, the relationship evolved into a true romantic bond.

Jeremy and Puddin were both twenty years-of-age when they decided to consummate their relationship.

They rented a cottage in the mountains where they would spend several days.

When the moment came for physical intimacy, Jeremy became increasingly nervous, not because it was his first time with a lady but because he must conceal his true identity.

As the moment became imminent a comedy of errors dominated.

Puddin made the first move by saying,

"Why don't you slip into your robe while I freshen up? I'll only be a minute."

"Oh, sure!", answered Jeremy.

Puddin retreated into the powder room. While in her absence, Jeremy became uncharacteristically frantic.

After donning his robe, he reached into his bag for his red makeup tube.

His nose, navel and nipples were the first to receive color, leaving the buttocks until last.

Puddin could be heard running the water followed by the brushing of her teeth.

Just before she emerged, she announced that she was coming out to be with him.

In haste, Jeremy attempted to turn the stick of red upon his buttocks when the tube broke in half, leaving long splotches of crimson upon the back of his legs.

As he realized his predicament, he reached up to his face only to smear the paint along the side and further down upon his belly toward the navel.

Just as Puddin open the door to enter into the bedroom, Jeremy leaped across the bed to turn out the bedside lamp.

"It's so dark! I can't see you!" exclaimed Puddin. "Please, turn on the light so that I don't stumble upon myself!"

"The light? I can't find the switch," answered Jeremy.

"Well, silly," said Puddin, "it's on the wall right behind you. Wait, I'll turn on the bedside lamp."

"No! Don't do that!" cried Jeremy.

"Why not? Aren't we the shy one!"

As she turned on the light, Jeremy leaped across the bed in a blur to unplug the lamp from its socket.

"What are you doing?" asked Puddin.

"I think it's more romantic to be in the dark, don't you?" replied Jeremy.

"No, I don't. I want to see who I am making love to! Here, I'll find the wall switch."

Puddin turns on the wall switch as Jeremy quickly ducks into the bathroom.

"Where did you go? Now, stop with these foolish games! I want to be with you! Snickers, come out right now!"

Puddin turned for a moment to activate the wall switch.

At that moment, Jeremy comes out of the bathroom, now wrapped in a towel around his midriff and walking backwards into the room. As he reaches the bed he continued to walk backward to the wall switch, turning it off, again.

The room became dark again.

"Snickers, what is the matter with you? Are you trying to make me want you more? That is not necessary."

Jeremy groped around until he found a chair pillow, using it to cover his front side, enough to hide his smeared navel and nipples. He did not realize the long smear running across the side of his face.

Puddin again turned on the bedside lamp, only to find a mess of a clown, standing half naked with a pillow in front of him and a red mistake all over.

"Snickers, what is going…"

Her excitement turns to dismay, "on?"

A long silence ensued.

"What is this? What is on your face? Snickers?"

Jeremy slowly brings the pillow down, revealing a belly covered in red convolution.

"I was going to tell you. I didn't know how."

"Tell me what? I don't understand!" said Puddin.

"Puddin, I'm not a real clown. My name…My name is Jeremy Bigham. I have come here from another dimension."

"What? Another dimension? Have you lost your mind? What is going on?"

"It's true. I am Jeremy, not Snickers. My father owns a circus in my world and I came here when I was nine-years-old through a portal in a circus tent, leading to this place, Clown World."

Puddin is in disbelief.

"No! It can't be! How can this happen? Tell me the truth. You are playing tricks, right? Snickers?"

Jeremy says nothing.

Puddin suddenly springs up and dons her robe.

She puts it on before grabbing her clothes and hastily stuffing them into her bag.

"No! Wait! Don't go! Puddin! Come on, let me explain!" pleaded Jeremy.

"I've heard enough! Let me go! I am not ready for this cruel joke!"

Puddin leaves the room, slamming the door behind her.

Jeremy is left, standing naked, humiliated and red.

Puddin could be heard in the cottage lobby calling on the phone for a cab to pick her up.

Jeremy attempts to put on his clothes before stubbing his toe in the dark.

"Ouch! Puddin! Puddin, come back!"

Before he could dress, a car could be heard, followed by the slamming of a door before taking off into the night.

Jeremy is all alone.

He turns out the light and weeps.

Chapter Three

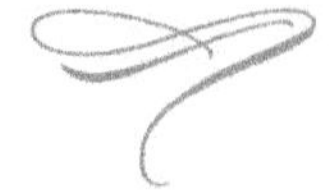

Puddin soon arrived at her family doorstep.

Her lashes were still wet from tears.

She retrieved her bag and headed up the porch steps, preparing to enter. Just at that moment, she heard a voice.

"Hey, Baby! What's new, Sugar?"

She turned to see what appeared to be Snickers, smiling and with provocative stance.

"Go away! I don't want to talk to you!" she exclaimed.

"Aw, what's the matter? Don't you like boys? Come on over here and let's talk."

"No! Go away!" says Puddin.

"Oh, come on. You don't mean that. Look, I have a car and lots of time.
Let's go get a soda at the arcade. How about it?"

"I told you NO, 'Jeremy Bigham, from another dimension'."

"What? Are you nuts? Who is this, 'Jeremy Bigham'? You have the wrong idea about me. I ain't gonna hurt 'cha. Come on!"

"I am not talking to you! You've already made yourself very clear," said Puddin.

"Huh? We just met. Give me a chance. You look lonely. I can fix that."

Puddin opened her door and slammed it behind her. The sound of a turning lock could be plainly heard.

"OK, then. Have it your way. You don't know what you're missing!" Puddin peers through the window shutters as 'Snickers' gets in his car and drives away.

"That's odd," thinks Puddin,

"I didn't know Snickers had a car. Why didn't he tell me before we left for the mountains in a cab?"

What Puddin had not realized is that this person was not the actual 'Snickers', but his parallel equivalent whose name was actually, Doogle.

He resembled Snickers in every respect except for his generally, crude demeanor.

Unfortunately, this would not be the last time Puddin would run into this person. Equally unfortunate for Snickers, this would not be the last time for him, either.

Chapter Four

Jeremy slept at the cottage that evening.

The next morning, Jeremy put on his robe to step outside.

There, Nature dominated landscape as trees bent forward as if to lend sympathetic ear.

Birds traded places between brushes as to deliver urgent messages.

Flowers danced slightly to breezes as if to signal need.

In everything, there dwelled both activity and stillness.

In between, Fascination replaced Question and Anguish vanished to Distraction.

Reality existed alongside Fantasy.

Since the death of Gramps, what Jeremy had been lacking was mentoring— someone other than his parents—someone who might lead intention.

So, he thought it beneficial to seek advice as to how he might direct his life.

A lead was found through the curator of the cottage where Jeremy was staying.

"Go, here," advised the curator.

He produces a travel brochure.

"They might have your answers," he said.

"Thank you," said Jeremy, "Thank you very much!"

The Quidd Chapel

Jeremy's cab to this place faced significant unicycle traffic delay.

It seemed everyone had reason to belong—to be present.

The reason for Jeremy's visit was important, expecting simple answers to complex questions.

Now having access to a source, Jeremy believed this attempt might prove beneficial toward the development of Jeremy's character, 'Snickers the Clown'.

Dexter and Sinister

This pair were between them a contradiction.

As Siamese twins, the two were inseparable, as Good and Evil can coexist as do familiar parlor-mates.

While one might agree, the other might emphatically disagree. Where there might be a contention of debate from one, the other might find none necessary.

Sinister was the first to speak.

"What is your quest?"

"What is the meaning of life?" answered Jeremy.

"Good question," retorted Dexter.

"Bad question," answered Sinister.

Skomorokha, a jester, was acting as a mediator.

He was dressed in skin-tight pants and wore a shirt with multi-colored, geometric patterns on the print.

He wore a tall, coned hat with an attached tassel. A small bell would ring upon the quick movement of the head.

His toes were curled up into a snail-like position inside his shoes.

Bells adorned his ankles and more were on his cuffs.

"That's a 'maybe' question," said Skomorakha.

"It might so be, then again, not," he continued.

"We agree," said Dexter and Sinister in unison.

There was a long period of dissertation without words. Smiles replaced drawing away and eyes avoided contact.

A disassembly of thought seemed eminent.

"What is your purpose?", asked Dexter.

"My purpose? To make…to make people laugh," replied Jeremy.

"That is your purpose? That?", said Dexter.

"If that were our purpose, we'd be laughing forever," said Sinister.

"Forever, if not longer." said Dexter.

Laugh, laugh, laugh.

"There is no no better quest," said Skomorokha.

"None. Then again, there might be a reason for laughter which is better than the laughter itself," he continues.

Yes. There might be. Then again, there might not."

"Yes. Not," said the pair.

"Maybe there is another reason for your question?", asks Sinister.

"There is no other reason," Jeremy replied.

"I just need an answer."

"An answer. He needs an answer. Ha! Ha! An answer!"

There was laughter all around. Jeremy remained serious.

"You want an answer. You came for an answer. Ha, ha, ha, ha!"

"Answers lead to more questions and we haven't time for those. We have only answers. Or, not," states Skomorokha.

"Speak! What is your question besides the one you

asked?" "Why am I here?" asked Jeremy.

"Why are you here? (Laugh). Why are you here?? (Laugh).

"You are here because you are here," (Laugh),

"or not."

Jeremy screams.

"Come on! What is this? All this vice versa,

versa vice, maybe, maybe not, crap. It's babble!" cried Jeremy. "I came for answers, not confusion!"

"Answers are often confusing, or not," said Dexter.

"Questions, even more so, or not,"

said Sinister.

"Put them both together and what do you have? I'll tell you…more questions…less answers."

"Or, not," said Dexter.

Sinister continues.

"The one with the most questions may also be the one with the least answers. And, the one with the most answers may also have the least questions."

"Or, not," said Dexter.

Jeremy became more and more bewildered.

This endeavor seemed not only to be a waste of his effort, but also a dangerous confound to his quest.

Because of a lack of discernment between fact and fiction, true and false, a chasm had separated him from complete or partial awareness.

In desperation, Jeremy decided he should abandon his inquiry.

"I'm sorry. I have made a mistake by coming here. I must depart, immediately," said Jeremy.

"Do as you must," said Skomorokha, "but do you hear that?"

"Hear what?" asked Jeremy.

"That sound," replies Skomorokha.

"What sound?"

"Do you not hear it? It grows louder as we speak," said Sinister.

"I hear nothing," replied

Jeremy. "He hears nothing."

All laughed.

"Do you not hear the train?" asked Dexter.

"The train? What train? I hear nothing but a bunch of hooey," said Jeremy.

"It comes closer. You must prepare to depart," said Skomorokha.

Jeremy asks, "Where does this train that you speak of originate and what is its destination?"

"It comes from there and stops here, where you are, then leaves here and stops there," said Dexter.

"And so, what does this train have to do with anything I have been asking?"

"Why, everything or…nothing. You must hurry. It's almost here!" said Dexter.

"Enough! There is no train," said Jeremy.

"Little faith that there is", said Dexter.

"Large faith that there is not", said Sinister.

"There is no reason for me to remain here," said Jeremy.

"On the contrary. It has everything to do with your being here," said Skomorokha.

"Or not," replied both clerics in unison.

Jeremy laughs.

"Then, what is this train called? The mystery train? The train to Hell?"

Skomorokha replies,

"The train is never expected when you choose it to be. As in Death, the train will in time, terminate."

"Then let it terminate. I"ll have no use for it!" said Jeremy.

"So you say, but just be aware of the consequences," said

Skomorokha. "What consequences?", asked Jeremy.

"Of your existence. The train is coming to consummate your existence," said Skomorokha.

Jeremy is indignant.

"Oh, really! So, I must heed this foolishness and follow your directives?"

"What you call foolish may be practical, especially by someone without enlightenment, as yourself," said Skomorokha.

Jeremy is confused.

"How does this make sense? How can I…what am I supposed to believe?"

"You mustn't believe before you trust. Trust comes first, or second, whichever comes first," replied

Sinister.

At that moment, a train whistle could be heard with screeching of brakes and hissing of steam. A male voice calls out—

"All aboard!"

"It's time," said Skomorokha.

"Do you have your ticket?"

"I have no ticket. I hadn't planned on travel beyond this place," said Jeremy.

"Without a ticket you must appeal to the graces of the engineer to allow travel without proper pass," said Sinister.

Dexter adds, "Or, you may stowaway, as does a hobo."

"I am no hobo! I am a gentleman of ethic and I choose to ignore this….train!", said Jeremy.

"Suit yourself," said Dexter.

"Perhaps you will change your mind when your past catches up with your present…or not," said Sinister.

"Yes. That could be so," agrees Jeremy, "or not."

Skomorokha said,

"Bravo! We think you finally have it! The paradox remains throughout infinity and you have accurately identified it! Congratulations!"

Jeremy listens.

"I have no idea what you are talking about. I'm leaving."

The Train to Baraboo

"Watch your step, please," said a man dressed in an awkward train porter uniform.

Jeremy makes one step out of this element and immediately onto the steps of a waiting passenger car.

"Easy. Take your time," said the porter.

"Where are we going? What is this train's destination?" asked Jeremy.

"Wherever you want. Where are you going?"

"I…I want to go home,"

replied Jeremy.

"Home? Home? You have a home? How special! Most have no home to call their own. We call this train, 'Home'. It's the only home we've ever known."

"We love to travel, you know, and this train takes us everywhere…wherever whim leads us. Haven't you a whim? Where's your home?" asked the porter.

"Baraboo. It is not of this world and neither am I," replied Jeremy.

The porter said, "That makes sense. Come on, let's go."

Before Jeremy could converse any longer, the train had begun to sputter forward.

Jeremy held onto the handrail as the porter hastened his advancement.

"Hurry, now. We must keep our schedule."

Jeremy boards.

Immediately, he observes that he is the only passenger on the train.

"Hello? Hello? Where is everyone?"

Another appearance of the porter.

"Tickets, please."

"I have no ticket. I am here by default," said Jeremy.

"And who has sent you?" asked the porter.

"Those…people, back there. They insisted I take this train."

"We know of no one. So, are you a stowaway?"

"Yes! Yes, I am a stowaway," said Jeremy.

"Very well. Have a seat. Enjoy the ride."

"But, where are we going?" he asked.

"You'll see. May I bring you a refreshment? A glass of ale, perhaps? Maybe a sandwich?"

Before he could say no, Jeremy's stomach growled from its emptiness. "Why, yes. That sounds nice. A sandwich and ale."

"Coming right up! Now, make yourself comfortable. The train will reach maximum speed before you know it!"

"That's nice, but where is it going?" Jeremy again inquired.

There was no answer.

The ale was cold and the sandwich was satisfying.

After eating, sleep soon came.

Slumber had replaced bruises incurred in travel and a wasting because of a lack of sustenance.

After an unknown period of time, Jeremy was awakened by a sudden jolt resulting from the hard application of brakes.

A voice announces, "Baraboo. All out!"

As it came to a stop, the engine spewed sooty confetti from its stack.

The caboose, being clearly dedicated through it's necessity, was content to follow the others closely by the tail, with iron chains insuring its firm, but flexible attachment.

"Baraboo?"

Jeremy looked out the window to see familiar buildings and activity.

People were clowns. All clowns.

As Jeremy gathered his wits, he stood from his seat and headed toward the exit.

"Have a nice visit!" saluted the porter.

"Thank you. I shall, Sir." answered Jeremy.

"Goodbye!", said the engineer.

"Goodbye!", answered Jeremy.

Suddenly, hundreds of passengers appeared from previously unoccupied seats.

In unison, they together emerged their heads through each train car window and said,

"Goodbye!"

They then returned as before, becoming spirits without matter.

The Clown Circus

Jeremy had wondered what the circus was like in this world.

He felt he knew these streets like the back of his hand as it shared similarities to the place he knew a short time before.

The difference between this and his home was that everything here was exaggerated.

Buildings had stripes and polka-dots. Sidewalks were motorized.

Street signs relayed multiple messages as to direction.

At street crossings, a questionnaire would determine whether the crosser is coming or going, or vice versa.

A quick hike should take him directly onto the circus grounds.

The Gigem and Runn Circus

"The sign must be wrong!," thought

Jeremy. "Like, who the blazes is, 'Gigem'

and 'Runn?'"

"I gotta see this!" thought Jeremy.

A brisk walk turned into a swift trot.

As he approached the main gate, Jeremy instinctively walks right in, passing the ticket booth.

"Hey! Hey, you!" says a voice

"Where's your ticket?"

"I have no ticket." answered Jeremy.

"Then you need me to give you one?"

"Yes, sir. I do!", said Jeremy

"OK. How much money you got?" asked the man.

"None, sir. I have none."

"Perfect! Here's your ticket. Go on in!"

So is the policy here.

Jeremy entered the circus gate.

Everything seemed strangely familiar to him, even though it wasn't entirely true to the natural place of his upbringing.

There, standing aside, was a female.

She appeared to be about Jeremy's age.

Her face closely resembled that of a camel.

Her attire was conservative, yet unflattering upon such a disproportionate torso.

A frozen scowl highlighted a chiseled brow and an awkward stance dominated her less-than-feminine carriage.

Noticeably large hands accompanied her oversized feet.

s Jeremy ponders her unusual appearance, her

mouth emits a squawk as does chalk upon a

blackboard.

 "Hey, Baby! Wanna get in my pants?", she retorted.

With genuine disdain for such crude advances, Jeremy decided to ignore her.

Suddenly, from under her dress, she produced a long vacuum hose bearing the name, 'Hoover'.

Its suction had a strong pull upon Jeremy's hair and clothing.

"You're cute! Marry me!" retorted the female.

"No! You're ugly! Stop!", cried Jeremy.

Upon that, the hose was retracted to be replaced by a baton, where she begins to beat Jeremy over the head.

 "Demon! You're a demon!", she cried.

Precisely then, Jeremy notices a pair of pants standing right beside him.

They were without any occupant, rather, they were full of unshelled peanuts.

Jeremy grabs a handful and proceeds into the circus.

A band was playing music from various acoustic instruments including trumpet, trombone, saxophone and clarinet, timbres we are familiar with.

Here, clarinets and saxophones were played by the constriction of the armpit upon the reed.

A calliope was in the stead of a piano.

Every player had the ability to hum along with their perspective pitches, creating unisons and harmonic counterpoint amongst the ensemble.

Tubas were not blown but rather, squeezed, in similar fashion to bagpipes.

A tuba player is mixing drinks for others by pressing down on the instrument's valves, dispensing alcoholic spirit and seltzer into cups.

A trumpet player is apparently half-awake, only gaining consciousness long enough to realize he's several measures late in the music and has missed most his entrances.

His partner tries to cover for him, only to have his dentures fly from the instrument's bell, landing on the firmament and chattering by themselves.

A trombone player had a boxing glove attached to the end of his slide, repeatedly hitting a bassoon player in back of the head as he transitioned between positions.

Jeremy's steps brought him to the place where he felt most adjoined, the clown tent.

And, as if by divine presence, the hole in the tent through whence he often peered was there.

There is much hurry and scurry—clowns following cue, preparing for performance.

Amidst this scene comes a familiar voice.

"Hello, Jeremy…I mean, Snickers!"

Jeremy turned to lay eyes on none other than Dynamo.

"Dynamo? Is that you?"

"The one and only!" answered Dynamo.

"Why…What are you doing here?"

"Why shouldn't I be here? Aren't clowns allowed to be where they belong?" said Dynamo.

"Where they belong? I don't understand. Shouldn't you…aren't you supposed to be in my Dad's circus?"

"Are you really our Dynamo, or are you an equivalent of this world?" asked Jeremy.

"It's really me, Son. There's much to explain, but right now I must get to my place. We'll talk later."

As quickly as he appeared, Dynamo was off again.

"Dynamo! Wait!", shouted Jeremy.

"Where are you going? Let me follow you! Dynamo!"

Dynamo disappeared into the crowd too quickly for Jeremy's easy pursuit.

Jeremy turned back to the clown tent to peer through the hole.

By this time, everyone had been called to the main tent, so it was largely empty.

There suddenly appeared another figure who was even more familiar than the last.

It was his father, Julius.

In this place, however, he possessed an uncharacteristically, jovial presence.

He was cordial and inviting where in our time, he would be just the opposite.

This 'Father' wore a brimmed hat, square toed boots and a vest with flashing lights.

Upon close inspection, these 'lights' were not electrical, but a matrix of live insects…fireflies, in fact.

As he spoke, the insects would undulate their beacons in perfect synchrony, chasing pattern and changing color.

Having noticed him, 'Julius' politely approached Jeremy.

"Hey! Hello! Who have we here? I haven't seen you here before. Are you new? Are you lost?"

"Hello, Sir!" said Jeremy.

As their eyes met, 'Julius', pondered Jeremy's face for the longest time before speaking again.

"You look familiar. Are you sure we haven't met? I usually become well acquainted with my clowns before their employ. Do you know your duties, here?" asked 'Julius'.

Jeremy answered, "Why, yes. I do!"

His harmonica was still in its vest pocket.

"Ah! A musician! Very well, then. Go and entertain your audience if that's what we've hired you to do! Quickly, now! Off you go!" said 'Julius'.

"Yes, sir! Right away!"

"Places!", shouted 'Julius'.

Employing his handy, Sengerphone, Jeremy noticed this device had lips and a tongue that moved as he spoke with teeth that brightly shined in their vicinities.

A mob of clowns was coming directly toward him, each encouraging the other to make haste to their assigned places.

"Come along! Let's go! Do not tarry! Hurry in order to make Mirth our immediate priority!"

Sounds of multiple, flopping pairs of oversized feet accompanied Jeremy's quick entrance into the ring.

The Sengerphone takes audience attention:

"And now…show your overwhelming appreciation for the most musical of clowns ever assembled under one tent. Maxie, Mitzy, Skinny and, um…"

He leans over to Jeremy and whispers,

"What's your name?"

"Snickers," replied Jeremy.

"…and Snickers, in their tribute to the music of the Ages! Take it away, Maestro," looking at Maxie.

They all look at Jeremy with his harmonica.

"Who is that?" asked Maxie to Mitzy.

"I don't know, but he has a harmonica," answered Mitzy.

"Whatever. Let's go!"

Jeremy had no idea of what tune was about to be performed. They simply nodded and began.

After only a measure or two, Jeremy picked up the melody of the selection. It was an atonal, yet rollicking polka featuring a drum, a tambourine, a zither and a trombone.

Jeremy instinctively took the musical lead.

His virtuosity was apparent, so the troupe allowed him to continue demonstration of his formidable, instrumental skills.

When time came for a singing interlude, the nod was also given to him which he flawlessly delivered with lyric and dance.

Smiles abounded throughout the tent.

The audience rose to their feet.

Thunderous applause nearly drowned the music as Jeremy continued with his ad-lib routine:

"Don't you just love us clowns?

The funniest clowns around…

We'll tickle your hearts before the next act starts and the corn pops in your shorts.

Don't you just love us clowns?

We're the craziest clowns in town.

When you need a tickle,

When you need a giggle,

It's us clowns who have the nickel."

Whatever the lyrics, they at least had a rhyme.

The clown troupe was in amazement over Jeremy's impromptu performance.

One of the members came up to Jeremy and asked,

"Where have you been? We've needed a fresh, comic mind for quite some time. There's something special about you, young man!"

"Why, thank you!" answered Jeremy.

Having no personal belongings aside from his harmonica the clothes on his back, Jeremy realized how he had no better place to be than here, as a clown in the circus.

But In the midst of his audience's adoration, Snickers the Clown suddenly felt alone.

He felt as an impostor; An alien from another world, but Human in all respects.

Puddin remained in his mind more each day. He wondered what had become of her.

It had been many months since they last met.

After the incident in the cabin, Jeremy believed that he shall never see Puddin again.

Nevertheless, he truly missed her company.

Sometimes, Jeremy would stop on the sidewalk in front of the old church and he would pray that she would someday return to him.

End of Season

Soon, the circus would begin its hiatus. The last performance would be two weeks from that day, on Sunday.

Jeremy would then celebrate his tenth month, sleeping on a cot in the clown tent, posing as a real clown in Clown World.

Although his reputation with the circus had grown, in two weeks he would become, essentially, unemployed.

Jeremy thought, "Money means nothing in this world. It's the keeping of The Child that's more important."

Jeremy had come to a point where he must choose what is acceptable to him, blending 'Child' with maturity of thought.

This would involve a reevaluation about who he really is who he has pretended to be.

The only people who were aware of his true identity would be Penelope, Mergetroid and of course, Puddin.

Jeremy began to long for his natural home with his sister and parents, but after a moments' consideration, he thought it best to wait just a while longer.

He didn't want to reveal himself in a manner which might cause any embarrassment to himself or others.

The Bowling Alley

That evening, Jeremy, went alone into a bowling alley. There, he found a small, dimly-lit bar, sat down on a stool and ordered a drink—a 'Kooky Kola.'

He just sat quietly, observing the activity.

Bowling in Clown World uses balls to knock down pins. However, both the ball and the pins are alive…animated.

Before choosing a ball, the bowler must address the ball.

"Hello, Ball!" would say the bowler.

"Hello, Champ!" answers the ball, only if the ball wants to be used by that particular bowler. If it doesn't want to be used, the ball would deliver a 'razzberry' sound through one of its finger holes.

The alive pins must grant their permission before any attempt is made to knock them down.

They are known to dodge incoming balls while laughing at their own antics. Noisy bunch, them.

Jeremy had taken only a sip of his drink when he spotted an envelope laying on the floor.

He looked around for someone who might have dropped it and saw no one.

Being unable to reach it from his stool, Jeremy got up picked the envelope from the floor.

He sat down, took one last glance around him and then looked back at the envelope.

It had been sealed with wax, but the seal had been broken. The imprint on the wax looked to be of a letter, 'P', in fancy script.

With curiosity getting the better of him, Jeremy removed the card from the envelope.

It appeared to be a wedding invitation, lettered in gold on the outside and with matching highlights throughout.

It read, "You are cordially invited to witness a Stupendous, Matrimonial Occasion."

"Hmm!", thought Jeremy. "Stupendous?"

Jeremy took another sip of his drink. He then proceeded to read the rest:

"Next Sunday…Puddin Pie is to marry Doogle Dandy, at the church, 3 PM."

Jememy choked, spitting out his drink.

"Puddin? And…"Doogle? She thinks he's ME!!"

"She was here! She was at the bowling alley. I must try to find her!"

Jeremy stuffed the card into his pocket, leaped from his perch and began to run toward the church. He briefly returned to snatch the bottle of pop from the counter, hastily gulping down the remainder.

After wiping his chin, he departs.

The Reception

In Clown World, wedding receptions occurred before the wedding, not after. So, most of the invited guests were already inebriated beyond civility before the wedding.

Confetti was on the floor and balloons floated near the ceiling.

Jeremy had to duck flying champagne bottles and glasses as he entered.

Everyone was singing and dancing wildly to the tune, 'Be a Clown'.

A bar had been erected on the alter.

There, Jeremy could see Doogle sitting with some guy friends, all getting plastered.

He scanned the room for Puddin and saw her conversing with other girls at a punch bowl.

As Doogle leaves to go to the restroom, Jeremy makes his move.

He walks up to Puddin's back, and says,

"Hello, Puddin."

Puddin turns toward him and says,

"Just a minute, Dear," thinking Jeremy was Doogle, and turns back.

Jeremy speaks again.

"Puddin, it's me…Jeremy Bigham."

Puddin slowly turns back around to face Jeremy.

"I'm Jeremy. Remember?"

"Oh, yes!" says Puddin. "Jeremy Bigham from another dimension! How could I forget?"

"Puddin, I have to talk to you," said

Jeremy. At that moment, Doogle

emerges from the restroom.

He sees Puddin talking to Jeremy and walks over to them.

"Puddin, who's this?"

He notices Jeremy's resemblance to him.

"Whoa! A twin! I didn't know I had a twin!" said Doogle.

"He's Snick…" Puddin corrects herself.

"He's Jeremy. Jeremy Bigham. He's from…"

Jeremy interrupts.

"I came from there and now I'm here," said Jeremy.

Doogle's facial expression showed skepticism.

Jeremy turned to Puddin, asking, "Can we talk?"

One of Doogle's drinking buddies came up, saying,

"Hey, Doogle. Come here. You have to see this!"

Doogle says, "OK, I'll be there in a minute."

He continues to eye Jeremy.

"Doogle, hurry up! You're gonna miss it!" said the buddy.

"I'll be right there," says Doogle as he heads back to the bar.

Jeremy took Puddin by the hand, leading her outside.

"Puddin, there's been some confusion."

She listens.

"I'm true," said Jeremy.

He continues.

"Puddin, I love you. I have always loved

you." She is confused.

"How can this be? It won't work!" said Puddin.

"You're from another dimension."

"That's right," replied Jeremy.

He paused.

"Come back with me!" he proposes.

"What? Come back with you to where?" she said.

"To my world," replied Jeremy.

"I'm not sure…" said Puddin.

By this time, Doogle was completely drunk.

"Come on. It's not very far away," said Jeremy.

"I can't believe this is happening!" said Puddin.

Jeremy spoke.

"Do you remember when we were kids, you always hung around. We were the best of friends."

Puddin smiled. "Yes, we were!"

"And you loved me then, I think," said Jeremy.

"Yes. Yes, I did." she replied.

"So what happened?" asked Jeremy.

"I don't know. I guess it was about your being from another dimension," she said.

Jeremy's head lowered in disappointment and he began to sob.

Puddin felt sorry for him. She produced a handkerchief for his nose.

As she rubbed, Jeremy's nose color became flesh.

She continued to wipe until all red was removed.

Doogle reappears, slurring his words.

"Puddin, what's going on?"

He sees Jeremy and came up to him.

"Hey! What is this?"

"Where's your nose?" asked Doogle.

"It fell off," said Jeremy.

"It fell off? How can a nose fall off?" said Doogle.

Laughing, he turns and falls flat on his back.

Puddin reacts.

"Disgusting. He's disgusting!"

"Tzen come with me, now," said Jeremy.

Puddin doesn't speak as she follows Jeremy into an alley.

At the end of the alley is the same brick wall he initially had come through.

He searched along with his hands to reveal the portal.

Together, Puddin and Jeremy went through.

Chapter Five

Passage through was easy enough.

Upon arrival they found themselves in an abandoned clown tent.

The main tent was gone but the house still existed.

Jeremy and Puddin' entered through a side door and walked to a landing near the main staircase.

"Hello, Jeremy," said Julius who was standing at the top of the staircase. He looked to be in very poor health.

"I knew you'd be back," he said.

"Father!" said Jeremy. "Yes, I'm back."

"I see you've brought a companion," said Julius.

"Yes," answered Jeremy, "this is Puddin."

"I welcome you to my abode," said Julius.

"Where's Mother?" asked Jeremy.

"Your mother is gone. She passed away several years ago."

Julius picks up a photo album.

"I want to show you something."

He turned to an old photo of his father and his mother who held a baby in her arms.

"This is the three of us in Clown World, many years ago," said Julius.

Jeremy is startled.

"Me? Why am I there?" asked Jeremy.

"You were born there," answered Julius.

"Born…in Clown World?" said Jeremy.

"That's right. That's your Mother, Jeremy. She was a real clown. That's makes you half-clown," explained Julius.

"Wow! But where is my red nose and…" asks Jeremy.

"You inherited my genes above your mother's, so you were born without any clown attributes," said Julius.

"Hello, Jeremy," said a stranger who was dressed in civilian clothes.

"Who are you?" asked Jeremy.

"Ha! Don't you recognize me?" Jeremy looks harder.

"I'm Dynamo! I'm out of my costume and make-up! My real name is Ben. Ben Harley."

"Dynamo, I mean, Ben? Weren't you just in Clown World?"

"Yes, I was. I can come and go as I please," he answered.

"But, are you not a real clown?" asks Jeremy.

"No, I'm not, but I like it there. I went back right after you entered. I was looking out for you," he said.

"But, Father, what were you doing there so long ago?" asked Jeremy.

Julius takes a moment to answer.

"I was scouting for talent. I'd find clowns with exceptional ability and bring them back to our circus."

"There is certainly a lot of talent there. We can go back and try to recruit more of the clowns…" said Jeremy.

"It's too late. The circus went bankrupt. I had the clown tent destroyed after you all returned," said Julius.

Jeremy looked out the door to see a bonfire which had already reduced the clown tent to cinders.

Chapter Six

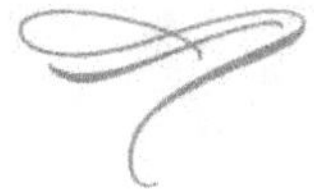

Julius passed within a year, leaving Jeremy and Puddin the house and empty grounds. They were married and had several children, all with clown attributes.

One can today find Jeremy's family together on a couch, children playing with his costume nose.

From out of nowhere comes a banana cream pie, which lands right in your face!

The End

Even though you're only make believing,

Laugh, clown, laugh!

Even though something inside is grieving,

Laugh, clown, laugh!

Don't let your heart grow too mellow,

Just be a real Punchinello, old fellow.

You're supposed to brighten up a place

And laugh, Clown, laugh!

Paint a lot of smiles around your face

And laugh, clown,

Don't frown,

And don't let the world know your sorrows,

Just be like Pagliacci and laugh,

Laugh, clown, laugh!

www.ingramcontent.com/pod-product-compliance
Lightning Source LLC
Chambersburg PA
CBHW071204300726

48975CB00004B/1281